MW00981208

GRACE
STREET
KIDS

*MEGAN &
THE OWL TREE*

GRACE STREET KIDS

MEGAN & THE OWL TREE

STANDARD
PUBLISHING
Cincinnati, Ohio

Marti Plemons

Grace Street Kids

Megan & the Owl Tree
Josh & the Guinea Pig
Georgie & the New Kid
Scott & the Ogre

Acquisition and editing by March Media, Inc.

The Standard Publishing Company, Cincinnati, Ohio.
A division of Standex International Corporation.

© 1992 by The Standard Publishing Company
All rights reserved.
Printed in the United States of America

99 98 97 96 95 94 93 92   5 4 3 2 1

Library of Congress Cataloging-in-Publication Data

Plemons, Marti.
  Megan & the owl tree / Marti Plemons.
    p. cm. — (Grace Street kids)
  Summary: When she finds that plans for building sidewalks in her neighborhood
will destroy many trees, one of which harbors a pair of nesting owls, sixth grader
Megan calls upon the help of God and the other kids of Grace Street.
  ISBN 0-87403-685-2
  [1. Conservation of natural resources—Fiction. 2. Environmental protection
—Fiction. 3. Owls—Fiction. 4. Christian life—Fiction.] I. Title. II. Title: Megan and
the owl tree. III. Series: Plemons, Marti. Grace Street kids.
  PZ7.P718Me 1992
  [Fic]—dc20   91-41593
                                                   CIP
                                                   AC

For Diane Jennifer

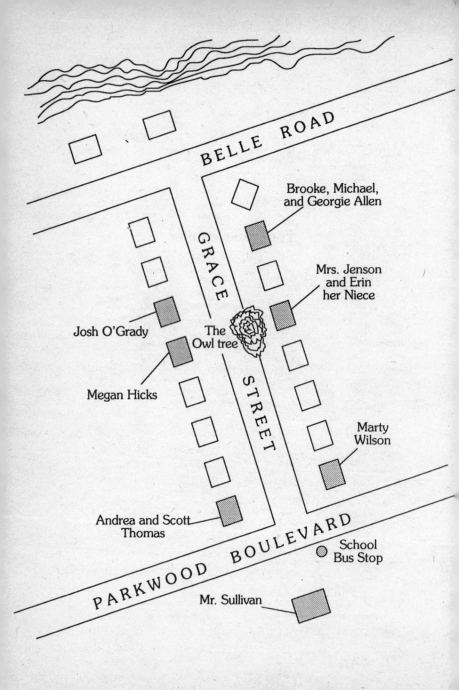

BELLE ROAD

GRACE STREET

Brooke, Michael, and Georgie Allen

Mrs. Jenson and Erin her Niece

Josh O'Grady

The Owl tree

Megan Hicks

Marty Wilson

Andrea and Scott Thomas

PARKWOOD BOULEVARD

School Bus Stop

Mr. Sullivan

Chapter One

Megan sat in the lower branches of the Owl Tree watching the blue and white city van move haltingly through her Parkwood neighborhood. Each time it stopped, two men in plaid shirts and heavy boots got out. While one of them looked through a tiny telescope atop a tripod, the other one walked down the street and watched for the first man to wave. Then they wrote things on maps. Sometimes one of them used a paint gun to put a bright orange

X on a tree before they picked everything up and started over in another part of the street.

"They'll be on Grace Street soon."

Megan jumped at the words and nearly lost her balance on the tree branch. "Josh O'Grady," she fussed as she frowned down at the top of his head, "why don't you stop sneaking up on people like that?" Josh was in her sixth-grade class at school. They had lived next door to each other since kindergarten, and since kindergarten he had been doing things to irritate her.

"What sneaking? I was just passing by." Josh didn't look at her as he pumped his skateboard and stepped back into a one-eighty spin.

"Well . . ." said Megan. The skateboard made so much noise on the pavement it really was silly to accuse him of sneaking up on her. "Maybe I wasn't paying much attention."

"Yeah, maybe you weren't," Josh grumped, but he didn't leave. He just kept riding back and forth on the street below, moving his skateboard in big figure eights.

Megan looked at the blue and white van again. Josh was right, it was almost to Grace Street now. "I wonder what they're doing," she said.

"Don't you know? They're building side-walks."

Of course Megan knew about the sidewalks. Everyone in the neighborhood knew that the city was finally going to build sidewalks in Parkwood subdivision. What she didn't know was what all that looking through telescopes and waving meant. And what were those big orange X's for?

She was about to ask Josh when he yelled, "I can't wait to get my skateboard on those new sidewalks." The he pushed off, sailing up Mrs. Jenson's driveway.

The big oak where Megan sat was across the street from her house, at the edge of Mrs. Jenson's front yard. By the time Josh had spun around at Mrs. Jenson's garage door and come back out to the street, Megan had dropped to the ground, her brown eyes flashing angrily.

"Josh O'Grady! You know you're not supposed to do that."

"Aw, the old crow's not even home."

"That doesn't make any difference, and don't call her an old crow!"

"I wasn't hurting her old driveway, and what's it to you, anyway, Megan Hicks?"

"I like Mrs. Jenson. Besides, you might scare the owls."

"You're the one doing all the yelling, Hiccups," said Josh, and took off down the street saying, "Hic, hic, hic . . ."

This year Josh thought it was funny to call Megan "Hiccups." Megan hated it, but she tried to ignore him.

She looked up into the Owl Tree. The huge oak towered over Grace Street, its branches spreading across to Megan's yard. Gray squirrels chased one another through the leaves, and way up at the top, so high that Megan couldn't see it from where she stood, was the owls' nest. At night Megan could hear them calling to each other, their gentle "hoo-hoo-hoo's" blending in perfect harmony.

Just then Brooke came around the oak's broad trunk, her head thrown back and her dark eyes straining to see through the leaves. "What are you looking at?" she asked Megan.

"I thought you were at dance class." Megan turned to smile at her.

"I was and now I'm home," Brooke explained. "What's up there? Flying saucers?"

"You wish," laughed Megan. They had been best friends in the whole world ever since Brooke's family moved to Grace Street three years before, but Megan still didn't know why Brooke loved all that outer space stuff so much.

"Yeah, I do wish," said Brooke, but she laughed, too.

"How many babies do you think the owls will have this year?"

"I don't know. Who cares?" Brooke plopped down on the ground with her back against the tree.

Megan sat beside her. "Well, don't you think the owls make Grace Street sort of, you know, special?"

"I guess so," said Brooke, but she was looking at something down the street. "Here they come."

Megan looked, too, and saw the city van coming around the corner onto Grace Street. "What are they doing?" she asked. "I mean, I know it's for the sidewalks, but what are they *doing*?"

"My mom says they're surveyors."

"What's that?"

Brooke shrugged. "I don't know exactly. We drove past them on the way home from dance class, and that's what Mom called them. I think it means they're figuring out where to put the sidewalks."

Megan thought for a minute. "They're spraying paint on some of the trees."

"I know," said Brooke. "Big orange X's all over the neighborhood."

"Me-gan!"

Her mom's voice came drifting across the street, and Megan stood up, dusting off the seat of her pants. "Guess it's dinner time. See ya."

Megan sprinted through the side yard but slowed down when she got to the back porch. Her dad didn't like for her to run in the house. She opened the kitchen door quietly and walked inside.

"Hi, sweetie," said her mom. "Wash your hands and set the table, please."

Megan liked having dinner with her family. They were always together for dinner, no matter what. If she spent the night at Brooke's house, she went *after* dinner. It was one of her dad's rules. Her dad was a lawyer and he had lots of rules, but Megan didn't mind. She sort of liked some of them.

Everyone helped put the meal on the table, even her sister Amy who was only five. Megan didn't have time to ask anybody anything until after the blessing had been said and her dad was spooning vegetable lasagna onto her plate.

"The surveyors are on Grace Street now," she said.

"Are they?" Her dad didn't sound very interested.

"What's a surveyor?" asked Amy.

Megan was hoping someone else would answer but nobody did, and Amy was looking right at her. "I don't know," she finally admitted.

Her dad laughed. "How do you know they're surveyors if you don't know what one is?" he asked.

Megan's face felt hot, and she paid a lot of attention to the Thousand Island dressing she was putting on her salad. "Brooke's mom called them that. I know they're for the sidewalks," she added.

"Right, as usual. How'd we end up with such a smart girl, Mrs. Hicks?"

Megan's mom smiled at her and turned to Amy. "Surveyors are the ones who figure out how much of our yards belong to the city," she said, "so they'll know where to put the sidewalks."

"How do they . . ." Amy's mouth was full of lasagna, and she stopped talking when she saw her mom frown at her.

"They look through little telescopes," said Megan.

"Right again," said her dad with a big smile. Megan suddenly felt much better. "Actually, it's more than just a telescope," he explained. "It's called a *transit*, but it does have a telescope on it."

"They look on a map," Megan's mom added, "and it tells them the boundary goes from here to here." She put her index fingers down at different places on the tablecloth. "They use the telescope to help them draw a straight line between the two places."

"Oh," said Megan. She thought a minute and had an idea. "Do they use the X's on the trees to help them see where the line should go?"

Her father answered, "Good try, Megs, but

they use stakes for that. Those X's are just so they'll know which trees to cut down later."

Megan dropped the piece of lettuce she was about to put into her mouth. "Cut down? Why do they want to cut down all those trees?"

"Because the trees will be in the way when they start to build the sidewalks," said her mom.

"Will the sidewalks go all the way to Josh's house?" asked Amy.

"And down the street and around the corner," said her dad.

"Will they let little kids ride tricycles on them?"

Mom laughed. "Yes, they will, but only to Josh's house and back."

Megan had to laugh, too, but she still didn't feel right about the trees. She didn't know whether to feel happy or sad about the sidewalks.

After dinner Megan and Amy cleared the table and loaded the dishwasher. Amy was chattering on about tricycles, but all Megan could think about was trees. The window over the kitchen sink faced the front yard, and Megan leaned over the dishwasher door to look at the Owl Tree. When she saw it, she almost dropped one of her mom's favorite bowls.

"No!" she cried, and ran to the front door to get a better look. A huge orange X marked the Owl Tree.

Chapter Two

At school the next day, Megan missed six words on a surprise spelling test. To top that, Mr. Vanatta said she had to do her science homework over, and science was her best subject!

"I thought today would never end," she told Brooke as they sat together on the bus that afternoon.

"I heard what happened at lunch," said Brooke.

Josh had called Megan "Hiccups" in front of the whole cafeteria. "It's not just that," said Megan. "I flunked a spelling test."

"So what? You're a lousy speller."

"I know, but I'm usually good at science and I messed that up, too. I'm just so worried about the Owl Tree. How am I supposed to think about school work?"

"If you lived next door to that tree," Brooke said, "and had to rake all those leaves and acorns, maybe you wouldn't be so sorry to see it go."

"We get leaves in our yard, too." Megan couldn't believe her best friend wasn't on her side.

Brooke didn't answer. The bus was almost to Grace Street and she was busy gathering her books and jacket. Megan picked up her books and followed Brooke off the bus. Walking toward home, she kept her eyes on the great spreading oak.

"Just look at it, Brooke. In the afternoon it shades our whole front yard. Mrs. Jenson says it's over two hundred years old."

"See if you can spend the night at my house this Friday," said Brooke, and Megan could tell

she didn't want to talk about the Owl Tree any more. "My little brother has this great new movie on tape about plant people from outer space."

"That movie isn't new," said Megan. Brooke may have been the one who knew about outer space, but Megan knew something about movies.

"Well, it's a new tape," said Brooke. "Michael just bought it. And, anyway, *I've* never seen it." They came to the Owl Tree and they stopped to look at each other. "So do you want to spend the night or not?"

"Sure," said Megan.

"Great!" Brooke smiled as she ran off toward her house. "See you later!" she called.

Megan looked at the bright orange X sprayed onto the rugged bark and tried to imagine Grace Street without the Owl Tree. No shade. No leathery brown leaves in autumn. Just a big hole in the sky. Where would the squirrels get their acorns for the winter? Where would the wood-peckers go to hammer out insects? What would happen to the owls?

Megan remembered watching three downy owlets learn to fly last summer. A tear slipped out and slid down her cheek. When she turned to brush it away, she noticed Mrs. Jenson sitting quietly on her porch swing.

"I know how you feel," said Mrs. Jenson softly. "It makes me want to cry, too."

Megan walked to the front steps and sat down. "Can't you stop them?" she asked. "It's your tree. How can they cut it down if you don't want them to?"

"I've tried to stop them," sighed Mrs. Jenson, "but, you see, it isn't really mine. It belongs to the city and they have the right to destroy it for a sidewalk." Mrs. Jenson shook her head slowly. "Two hundred years of tree for a few square feet of concrete."

"There must be *something* you can do!"

"Pray, dear, pray," Mrs. Jenson said. "It's all any of us can do."

Megan nodded and started down the walk. She wished she had told Mrs. Jenson that she *had* been praying, ever since the whole thing began. She looked back, but Mrs. Jenson had gone inside. Megan walked slowly across the street to her house. Her mom was in the kitchen.

"Hi, sweetheart, have a good day?"

It was what her mom always asked when she

came home from school, or when Megan's dad came home from work and, probably, when Amy came home from kindergarten. Another thing she said was, "If you expect a good day, you'll have a good day."

"It was a terrible day," said Megan.

Her mom put down the knife she had been using to chop carrots and looked at Megan carefully. "Want to talk about it?"

"Mom, why do we have to have sidewalks?"

"You know the answer to that, Megan. It isn't safe for you children to be walking in the streets."

"But we always watch for cars."

"I know you do, honey, but what about the little ones like Amy? They don't always remember."

Megan nodded. She knew the sidewalks were a good thing, but so were the trees.

"Here," said her mom, and handed her a carrot.

Megan started to her room but had to come back when her mom called, "Take your things with you, please." She grabbed her books and went down the hall. By the time she had tossed them onto her bed, Amy was at her door.

"Hi, Megan, did you have a good day? Can I have a bite of your carrot?"

"Yes, you may." Megan handed her the carrot. "In fact, you can have the whole thing. I don't want it."

"Thanks!" said Amy and took the carrot as if she couldn't believe her good luck. After she had taken a big bite, she asked again, "Did you have a good day?" Now Megan was sure her mom said that to Amy, too.

"No," said Megan, "I had a terrible day, and don't talk with your mouth full."

All the smile went out of Amy's face and her lower lip began to pooch out. "You mad at me, Megan?"

Megan wished Amy would just go away and leave her alone. "No, Amy, I'm not mad," Megan tried to make her voice soft. "I just have a lot of things to do tonight. Why don't you go play in your room?"

"You sound mad."

"I'm not mad," she said. But she realized Amy was right—she did sound mad. "Well, maybe I am mad, but not at you, OK?"

"Who are you mad at?"

Megan thought a minute. "I don't know. The city, whoever that is."

"You're mad about the Owl Tree, aren't you?" said Amy.

"Yes, I am, but mostly because nobody can do anything to stop them, not even Mrs. Jenson." Megan thought about the SPEED LIMIT—15 MPH sign on the corner. Mrs. Jenson had written so many letters and made so many phone calls about cars speeding on Grace Street that the city had finally come out and put up that sign. "If Mrs. Jenson can't do it, nobody can," she sighed.

"Last Sunday Miss Lynch said God can do anything." Miss Lynch was Amy's Sunday school teacher.

"Miss Lynch is right," said Megan, "and I have been asking Him to do something to save the Owl Tree."

"Then He will," said Amy brightly.

Megan smiled at Amy. She knew that God always answered her prayers, but she also knew He didn't always give her the answer she wanted. Amy didn't know that yet.

"Megan! Telephone!" called her mom, and Megan hurried down the hall to the den.

It was Brooke. "We've got to get even with Josh," she said. "Now he's calling me Brooksie."

"That's better than Hiccups," said Megan.

"Let's see. Josh O'Grady. What can we call him that he'll hate?"

Megan didn't think God wanted kids getting even. "Mom says if we just ignore him, he'll get tired of it and quit."

"How about Joshie? Or Hogwash! What do you think? Hogwash Josh!"

"I don't know."

"You're thinking about that stupid tree again, aren't you?" said Brooke.

Megan wanted her to understand. "You know how much you love outer space?" she asked Brooke. "That's how much I love the Owl Tree."

"Oh," said Brooke, and Megan could tell she wasn't angry anymore. Brooke thought for a long time and said, "Then why don't you do something?"

"Do what? Even Mrs. Jenson couldn't get them to change their minds. If she couldn't do anything, what can one kid do?"

"Two kids," said Brooke.

Megan felt a little better. She didn't like it when Brooke wasn't on her side, but she couldn't see how it changed anything else.

"OK, two kids," she said. "What can two kids do?"

"I don't know. Maybe we can think of something. Did you ask your mom about Friday night?"

"Not yet."

"Well, don't forget," said Brooke.

"Are you kidding? And miss plant people from outer space?"

Brooke laughed. "You want to ride bikes? We could get in Josh's way and watch him get mad."

"Can't," said Megan. "I've got too much homework."

"Oh, yeah, Mr. Vanatta. Well, I'd better go. See you tomorrow."

"Bye."

Megan hung up the phone and went back to her room. She opened her science book and stared at the words, but she was thinking about the Owl Tree. "God," she prayed, "don't let them cut down the Owl Tree." She didn't know what else to say. God already knew how much she loved the old oak, and she knew how much God loved her. *He won't let them cut it down,* she told herself. *He just can't.*

Chapter Three

On Friday, Brooke ate dinner with Megan's family. Megan's dad had made little individual pizzas from his special recipe and everyone got to add their own toppings before putting the pizzas into the oven. Amy put pineapple and broccoli on hers.

"Yuck!" said Megan and Brooke at the same time.

"Bread-and-butter," said Brooke quickly.

31

"That's when you walk around two different sides of something," Megan told her.

"Well, what's for saying the same thing at the same time?"

"Cowabunga!" said Megan's dad, and everyone laughed.

Then he asked, "You don't think you kids invented that word, do you? They used to say *cawabonga* on the Howdy Doody show. It was spelled a little differently then, but *cowabunga* is older than I am."

"And that's pretty old," said Megan's mom. Mr. Hicks threw an oven mitt at her, but she ducked. It bounced off the side of Brooke's head.

After dinner, when Megan and Brooke were helping to clear the table and load the dishwasher, Brooke said. "You're so lucky."

"Why?"

"My dad would never throw an oven mitt at my mom."

"I like your dad," said Megan.

"He's OK, but I bet he's never even heard of *cowabunga!*"

"I'll bet he has," Megan countered. "Your dad knows lots of things."

Megan was sure Mr. Allen must be about the smartest man in the world. He taught history at the university, and Megan's own dad attended his Sunday school class at church. Once, when all the families on Grace Street had gotten together for a cookout, Mr. Allen had beaten everyone at Trivial Pursuit.

Megan had an idea. "I bet he would know what to do about the Owl Tree."

"Maybe," said Brooke, "but he was pretty happy about the sidewalks."

"So?"

"So I think he'd rather have sidewalks than trees."

Suddenly Megan felt miserable. Why did it have to be trees against sidewalks? *Why doesn't God do something?* she thought. But whose side was God on when both sides were good? Maybe *that* was what she would ask Mr. Allen.

It was dark when they walked to Brooke's house, and the old oak was just a huge shadow in the sky. "Listen," Megan whispered. Brooke stopped talking and tilted her head to the side. Coming from high in the branches was a gentle "hoo-hoo-hoo."

"It's the owls," said Brooke. "What . . ."

"Shh. Listen."

As they listened, a second voice joined in, its hoo-hoo-hoo's pitched slightly higher than the first. Brooke drew in a long, deep breath, and a smile spread across her face as she looked at Megan.

"They're harmonizing!"

Megan nodded. "Mrs. Jenson says their harmony is perfect."

When they got to Brooke's house, her brother was using the VCR. "Ten minutes," he said. Michael never said much. He was tall and dark like Brooke, and was usually so quiet that you could almost forget he was around—not at all like his sister.

Megan followed Brooke to the kitchen, where Brooke's mom was finishing up the dishes.

"Hi, girls."

Brooke said, "Hi, Mom," just as Megan said, "Hi, Mrs. Allen." Then they looked at each other and said, "Cowabunga!" at exactly the same time, which made them both start laughing.

Brooke's mom laughed, too. "You girls have the sillies tonight," she said.

"It's because we haven't had dessert yet," said Brooke.

"Oh, I see," said Mrs. Allen. "Well, I'm afraid we don't have much to offer here—just some plain old chocolate ice cream and some boring peanut butter cookies."

"We'll take it!" said Brooke, and Megan grinned. Mrs. Allen made the best peanut butter cookies in the world.

After cookies and ice cream, they went into the den and settled down to watch Michael's movie.

"Where's Georgie?" asked Megan. Brooke's younger sister was usually hanging around, trying to join whatever they were doing.

"She's spending the night at Marty's house." Martha Wilson lived at the corner of Grace Street and Parkwood Boulevard. She was Georgie's best friend.

While Brooke was talking, her dad had come into the den and retrieved his glasses from the table beside Megan. "Hi, Mr. Allen," she said, smiling up at him.

"Hello, Megan. You ladies have a big evening planned?"

Megan liked the way he always called them ladies. "We're going to watch plant people take over the world," she told him.

"Oh, dear," he said. "Brooke hasn't got you hooked on that sort of thing, too, has she?"

"It's just for fun," Megan laughed. "You want to watch it with us?"

"No, thank you. I have some reading I need to do. You'll have to tell me all about it later."

"OK."

Megan wanted to ask him her question, but Brooke already had the tape in the VCR and was starting the movie. The plant people came and the brave earthlings fought them off, and, in the end, nobody was exactly sure where the plant people had come from or whether they would be back some day.

"Why is it always like that?" asked Megan.

"Like what?" said Brooke.

"Why is it always we have to kill them or they will kill us?"

"It's just a movie."

"I know," said Megan, "but don't you wish just once they'd figure out a way that both sides could get what we wanted?"

"I like the way you think, Megan," said Mr. Allen. Both girls turned to find him standing in the doorway. "I'm supposed to remind you two not to stay up too late," he continued.

"Mr. Allen," said Megan, "can I ask you something?"

"Certainly," he said as he came into the room and sat on the arm of the sofa.

"It's about the sidewalks," she added.

"Brooke says you're worried about that big, old oak."

"The Owl Tree," said Megan. "I mean, I know the sidewalks are a good thing, but the owls . . ."

"Did you know they sing in perfect harmony?" asked Brooke.

Her dad smiled at her. "Seems like I read that somewhere," he said, "but I never really thought about it."

"Why do we have to choose between the owls and the sidewalks?" asked Megan.

"Life isn't easy, Megan." Mr. Allen's voice was as soft and gentle as an owl's. "Sometimes the questions are tough, and it's hard for us to know the right answers. That's when we have to trust God to show us what is right."

"But I have asked God to help. Why doesn't He do something?"

Megan looked away from Mr. Allen's clear, blue eyes. She was afraid he would tell her it meant that God wanted the sidewalks, too. But he said, "Maybe He needs some help this time."

Megan glanced up quickly, but Mr. Allen's face didn't look as though he were teasing. "Why would God need help?" she asked him.

"God moves in a mysterious way," he quoted. "He doesn't always do things the way we think He will. I suppose He could just reach down and solve all our problems for us if He wanted to, but I think He'd rather we did some things for ourselves."

"But how are we supposed to know what to do?" Megan asked.

"He'll show you, but first you have to show Him that you are willing to do your part."

"I'll do anything!" said Megan eagerly. Then she remembered her question, "But what if God wants the sidewalks?"

"God wants what's good."

"I know," Megan persisted, "but what if both things are good? What does He want then?"

"Think about your movie, Megan, and what you were saying when I came in just now."

Megan looked at Brooke. "What was I saying?"

Brooke frowned a little. "I think you were talking about both sides getting what they wanted."

"But how?" Megan repeated as she looked to Brooke's dad for the answer.

"I don't know," he said, "but I'm sure God does. Why don't you ask Him?"

Mr. Allen went upstairs to bed after that, and Megan and Brooke prowled around the kitchen for something to eat. They took their snacks to Brooke's room, but Megan discovered she wasn't very hungry after all.

"I've been thinking," she said. "In the movies, when they want to stop something from happening, they always start a petition."

"What's a petition?" Brooke asked.

"It's a piece of paper that everyone signs."

"What does it say?"

"I don't know, but it always seems to work." Megan thought about petitions for a minute. "Even if we could start a petition," she said finally, "nobody would sign it because everyone wants the sidewalks."

"Not everyone," said Brooke, but she didn't sound too sure.

"Oh, I hate sidewalks!" said Megan suddenly. "And I hate surveyors and I hate their stupid straight lines!" Then she stopped, and her frowning face slowly broke into a broad smile. When she looked at Brooke her eyes were shining. "That's it!" she said. "Brooke, that's it!"

"What's it?"

"I know how we can have sidewalks and not cut down the Owl Tree!"

Chapter Four

"Curvy sidewalks?" said Brooke's mom when they told her their plan at breakfast the next morning.

"I've seen curvy sidewalks," said Brooke's dad, "when I was in Atlanta last year."

"Really?" asked Megan.

Mr. Allen nodded. "I would imagine they're more expensive to build, though. The city isn't going to like the idea of paying extra money for our sidewalks."

"But it's for the trees," said Brooke.

"And the owls," Megan added, "and for all the other animals that need the trees."

"Put all that in your petition," said Mrs. Allen, "and I'll be the first one to sign it."

Glancing sideways at Megan, Brooke said, "We thought maybe you would help us write it."

Megan agreed. "We're not sure what a petition is supposed to say."

"It's easier to write than you think," said Mr. Allen. "You just say what you want the city to do and why. Then you get people who agree with you to sign it."

"We want curvy sidewalks," said Brooke.

"So they won't have to cut down the trees," said Megan.

"Then that's what you put in your petition," said Mr. Allen.

"After you finish your breakfast," Mrs. Allen added.

Later, in Brooke's room, Megan chewed the eraser on her pencil and stared at the long, lined yellow sheet of paper in front of her. Brooke leaned over the desk and watched her with great interest. They stayed that way for a full minute, until Brooke's dad stuck his head in the door and asked, "How's it coming?"

Brooke and Megan looked at each other, then turned to face him. "I don't know how to start," said Megan.

Mr. Allen walked over to the desk saying, "Let's see what you've got so far." He smiled when he saw the blank page. "Try this," he said, taking Megan's pencil and leaning over the yellow paper. On the top three lines he wrote: "I am *against* tree removal to make room for sidewalks. I am *for* making the sidewalks circumvent the trees." *Circumvent* had to mean "go around," Megan decided.

Mr. Allen numbered the rest of the lines to the bottom of the page, one through thirty-two. "You ask each person who agrees with you to sign his or her name and address on a numbered line," he explained. "And I'll be the first," he added, placing his name on the line numbered one. "I don't know if the city will go for it, but I certainly think it's worth a try."

"What do we do with the petition after everyone has signed it?" asked Brooke.

"We'll take it to city hall," said her dad, "and hope the city council will be impressed."

"Thirty-two isn't very many names," said Megan. "Can we number more pages?"

"As many as you like," said Mr. Allen. "Just copy those sentences at the top of each page."

"Great!" Megan said as she tore some sheets off the pad for Brooke. "We'll get the whole neighborhood to sign them. *That* will impress the city council. Thanks, Mr. Allen."

"Thanks, Dad," said Brooke. She took one of the sheets, skipped three lines, and started numbering. "You copy, I'll number," she told Megan.

"You're welcome, ladies, but remember to keep your numbers consecutive."

"Consecutive?" repeated Brooke.

"I think that means one after the other," said Megan.

"Right," said Mr. Allen. "Page two should start with number thirty-three."

"Oh," said Brooke, and crumpled the sheet she had been working on into a ball.

Mr. Allen laughed and patted her on the back. "I'm proud of you two," he said. "The petition was a wonderful idea."

The girls worked until Megan's mom called her home later that morning. They had copied and numbered twenty sheets. "I guess that's enough for now," said Megan.

When she showed the petition to her dad, he flipped through all the pages and whistled softly. "You and Brooke have been busy."

Megan felt proud and a smile slipped onto her face. "Yes, sir, and right after lunch we're going to start getting people to sign it."

"Looks like you've already started," he said. Mrs. Allen had signed line number two, right under Mr. Allen's signature. "Where's your pencil? I'll be number three."

Megan's mom signed the fourth line and helped Amy put her name and address on the fifth. "Can kids sign a petition?" asked Megan.

"Sure they can," said her dad, so Megan signed the next line.

"Brooke and Michael and Georgie will be three more," she said. "That's nine names already."

"Just don't expect too much, Megs," said her dad. "Some people might not want to sign."

"I know," said Megan, but she really believed everyone would want to save the trees.

"I just want you to be prepared," he said, "in case it doesn't go exactly as you planned."

"I'll be prepared," she promised.

"Even if someone laughs at you?"

Megan thought of Josh O'Grady. She would try him first, and if he didn't laugh, no one would. And if he did laugh, she knew she could handle it. "I'll be OK," she said.

Megan found Josh skateboarding in his driveway. "What you got there, Hiccups?" he called when he saw her coming.

"It's a petition," said Megan. "You want to sign it?"

"What's it for?"

"Curvy sidewalks," she said, and waited to see if he would make fun of her. Instead, he let out a whoop.

"Great idea!" he said. "Where do I sign?"

Megan stared at him. "You like the idea?"

"Sure! Just think how much fun it would be to skateboard on those babies!"

Megan had to smile at the thought of Josh speeding along the sidewalks, skidding around the trees, whipping past anyone or anything that got in his way. There was something else,

though, that made her smile just a little bit wider. Josh hadn't laughed. She felt like hugging him, almost. Instead, she got his name and address on the petition. Then she went inside with him to ask his mom and dad to sign.

Josh's dad was a big man with round, red cheeks and twinkling green eyes. Megan thought he would look like Santa Claus if he had white hair instead of the fiery red kind that all the O'Gradys had. His full, bushy beard had some strands of gray, but that was all.

"So Megan Hicks is getting into politics," he said when Megan showed him the petition.

Megan was still smiling from the good luck she had had with Josh. "Just to save the trees," she told him.

"An activist, then," he said. "I believe that's even worse." His voice was stern, but he gave Megan one of his famous winks and she knew he was only teasing.

"What's that?" she asked.

"An *activist*?" he said. "That's someone who fights for causes. Your cause is to save the trees."

"One tree, really," Megan admitted. "The Owl Tree."

"Ah," said Mr. O'Grady, his voice sounding soft and approving. "The Owl Tree, is it?" Megan nodded. "Then it's a cause from the heart, and I guess I'll have to sign in that case."

Megan left the O'Gradys with three more signatures on her petition. Josh went back to his skateboard. Megan waved to him and headed for Brooke's house. She felt good, really good. She felt all light and airy inside, because for the first time since the appearance of that hateful, orange X on the trunk of her beloved Owl Tree, Megan felt there really might be something one kid could do. *No, two kids*, she told herself as Brooke came bounding down the front steps to meet her.

"Dad gave us a clipboard and some extra pencils."

"That's great," said Megan. "Where do you want to start?"

"How about Mrs. Jenson? We know she'll sign it."

"OK, let's go." They started off across the yards and Megan added, "But I think everyone will sign it, don't you?"

"I don't know," said Brooke. "My dad gave me

one of his don't-get-your-hopes-up talks before I left the house."

"So did mine, but Mr. O'Grady said it was 'a cause from the heart.' Don't you love it? 'A cause from the heart.'" Megan said it again because she liked the way it sounded.

Mrs. Jenson was delighted to sign the petition, and she wished the girls luck. The Dickersons, Mrs. Jenson's neighbors, weren't home. "We'd better make a note so we'll remember to come back later," said Megan.

Brooke pulled a blank sheet from the back of the pad and started a list. By the time they had been to every house on Grace Street, there were as many names on the not-at-home list as there were on the petition. Megan sighed. "Let's try Belle Road next. Maybe somebody will be home over there."

"I think we should split up," said Brooke.

"Good idea." Megan took some of the petition sheets. "You take the houses on one side of the street and I'll take the houses on the other side. That way we'll get through twice as fast."

The plan worked. They did move faster, but the farther they went down Belle Road, the fewer people there were who knew them, and the more lectures they got about higher taxes and how silly curvy sidewalks would look. Still, most people agreed to sign the petition.

"Why not?" said one woman. "The city won't do it, anyway."

When she met Brooke at the far end of Belle Road, Megan's good mood had completely disappeared. "If the city won't do it, anyway," she complained, plopping down under a tree marked with a bright orange X, "why are we wasting our Saturday on this petition?"

"What do they know?" said Brooke. "They told me the same thing, but they signed it. So who cares what they think?"

Megan grinned up at her. "I told my dad I wouldn't be upset if they said stuff like that."

"So don't." Brooke grinned, too, and held out her hand. Megan grabbed it and pulled herself up. "We've still got lots of streets left, and look at all the names we've already got."

"We can make more sheets and take them to school Monday." said Megan. "I bet all the kids will sign."

"The teachers, too."

They crossed the street and started down Amanda Avenue, Brooke going to one side and Megan to the other, and with every step, Megan felt better and better.

Chapter Five

Sunday morning was sunny and warm, warmer than usual for the middle of April. Riding to church, Megan looked at the trees with birds in their branches and bright orange X's on their trunks. *Don't you worry,* she thought. *We've got a petition.* To her, the word *petition* seemed almost magical, promising protection for the trees of Parkwood subdivision.

Megan told her Sunday school class about the petition, and they all wanted to sign it. Her teacher, Mrs. Farmer, signed it and said she was proud of Megan and Brooke for what they were doing. "In fact," she said, "I'd like to talk about this some more, instead of what I had planned for this morning." She had everyone look up Psalm 24:1 and asked Megan to read it aloud.

"The earth is the Lord's, and everything in it," Megan read, "the world, and all who live in it."

"The earth is the Lord's," repeated Mrs. Farmer, "and He put it into our keeping. God wants us to take care of this beautiful world He has given us. He wants us to protect it, and that's what Brooke and Megan are trying to do with their petition."

The class spent the whole time talking about saving the trees, about recycling paper and plastic and aluminum, about not wasting things like water and electricity, and about picking up trash whenever you saw it lying around on the ground.

That afternoon Megan and Brooke went back to the houses on their not-at-home list. Josh O'Grady followed them on his skateboard, zipping into the driveway and out again at each place they visited.

"If it will keep that young man off my driveway with that thing," said Mr. Dickerson, "I'll be more than happy to sign it."

"I'm sorry about Josh," said Megan as she handed him the clipboard.

"It isn't your fault," said Mr. Dickerson. "It isn't his fault either, for that matter. Where else has he got to ride, except in the street? It's just that those wheels can do a lot of damage to my concrete."

Megan and Brooke waited on the porch while Mr. Dickerson went inside to get his wife's signature for them. "I wish Josh would go home," said Megan.

"I don't know," said Brooke. "I think he's good for business."

"What do you mean?"

"They all want to sign the petition just to get rid of him."

The girls were laughing when Mr. Dickerson came back, and Megan had a hard time stopping long enough to thank him. "This is supposed to be serious," she told Brooke after he had closed the door. But they laughed some more as they went down the porch steps.

They finished the list and found most of the people home this time, many outside enjoying the warm, spring day. Just about everyone signed the petition, and so they went to Megan's house to make more pages to take to school.

Monday morning, Brooke and Megan were the first ones at the bus stop. "Let's show it to Mrs. Leatherby first," said Megan, "and she'll probably take time for the whole class to sign it."

"Just like Mrs. Farmer did," agreed Brooke.

Mrs. Leatherby smiled when they showed her the petition, and took time to read it carefully. But she said, "I'm sorry, girls, but it's against the rules to circulate a petition on school property."

"Against the rules?" said Megan.

"I'm afraid so." She handed the pages back to Megan and added, "I'm sorry. You've done a good job, and I think it's a very good cause."

Megan thought, *a cause from the heart*, and almost cried standing right there at the front of the classroom with the whole sixth grade watching. She hurried to her seat and slumped down so Mrs. Leatherby couldn't see her face.

"What's the matter, Hiccups?"

Even though Josh had called her Hiccups, the

look on his face said he really did want to know what was wrong. "We can't ask anybody to sign the petition at school," she told him.

"Ask them to take it home and sign it."

"It's the asking that's against the rules."

"No problem," said Josh. "You got plenty of pages to that thing?"

Megan held up the petition to show him, but she couldn't ask any questions because Mrs. Leatherby was calling for everyone's attention. Josh just smiled. Megan looked at Brooke, who only shrugged, so she put the petition in her notebook and tried to pay attention to spelling.

At lunch, kids started coming up to Megan and asking for pages of the petition. "Give me a couple," said Jeffrey Tucker, "and I'll ask around my neighborhood."

"How did you know?" said Megan.

"Josh told me."

Megan handed him two numbered pages. "We need them back tomorrow." she said. "The city council meets tomorrow night."

"I'll do it this afternoon," he promised.

By the time the bus let them off at Grace Street, Megan and Brooke had given out all the extra

pages they had for the petition. "If they fill all those up," said Brooke, "the city council will really be impressed."

"And they'll *have* to agree to keep the trees then," added Megan.

"And make curvy sidewalks," shouted Josh, as he sailed down the street on his skateboard.

"I wonder why he helped us like that?" mused Brooke.

"Josh is OK," said Megan. "I don't think he means to make us angry all the time."

"Then why does he do it?"

"Mom says he just wants attention, you know, because he's an only child."

"But that means he already gets all the attention. Why's he trying so hard to get more?"

"Maybe he never learned how to share."

Brooke looked at Michael and Georgie who were walking ahead of them and said, "Yeah. I guess you could kind of get used to being the only kid around."

"I guess so," agreed Megan, "but I bet it's lonely sometimes."

Josh roared toward them on his skateboard, spun around and rolled up behind them. "Hey,

Hiccups," he said. "We going out again this afternoon? You know, with the petition?"

"Later," said Megan. "We have to make more pages first."

"Oh? What happened to all those pages you had at school this morning?"

"You know what happened to them," said Megan, walking backward so she could see his face.

Josh tried to make himself look innocent. "How should I know?" he asked. And before she could answer, he flipped Brooke's hair and took off again saying, "See you later, Brooksie."

"Not if I see you first," said Brooke, but not loud enough for Josh to hear.

They went to Megan's house to work on the petition. When her mom asked, "Did you girls have a nice day?" they both agreed they had, even though it hadn't started out that way.

They were able to fill two more pages and part of a third before supper, and on Tuesday, most of the kids who had taken pages remembered to bring them back. After school, Brooke went to Megan's house to help her sort the pages so the numbers would be right.

"Are you scared?" asked Brooke.

"Are you?"

"Yes."

"Me, too," said Megan, and the air in her lungs came out in a rush. "My dad said he would go with me, but I have to do the talking because it's my petition."

"That's what my dad said."

"You ever been to a city council meeting?"

Brooke shook her head and her long, black hair tumbled across her shoulder. "Have you?"

Megan said, "I've never even been to city hall before."

"I don't even know where city hall is," said Brooke.

Megan looked at Brooke's pale, serious face and burst out laughing. Brooke managed to spurt, "That . . . wasn't . . . funny," before the giggles got her, too.

"I know," howled Megan as she fell back onto the bed holding her sides.

"Do I detect a little nervous laughter back here?" Megan's mom was smiling as she came into the room.

Megan sat up on the bed, but she wasn't able to stop laughing right away. Brooke poked her with an elbow, and Megan poked her back. Megan finally managed to say, "Is that why we're laughing when it isn't really funny?"

Her mom nodded. "Yep. Your body is just trying to release a little tension. Are you girls all set for tonight?"

Megan wiped her face on her sleeve. "I think so."

"Great, Brooke, your mom called to say dinner's about ready. Tell her we'll will be ready to leave about 6:15."

To Megan, it felt like the trip to city hall lasted an hour, but she knew it really only took ten minutes. Walking into the council room, she slipped her hand inside her father's, and he gave her fingers a little squeeze. They walked to a bench near the front and sat down.

Megan was surprised to find the room almost empty and all the chairs vacant behind the long, shiny conference table. She leaned over and whispered to her dad, "Where is everybody?"

"They'll be here," he said. "The Allens just thought we should get here a little early."

"That way, you and Brooke can get used to the room before the meeting starts," said Mr. Allen.

Megan and Brooke were sitting in the middle, between their families. As Megan looked around at the old polished wood and the warm brass lamps set along the walls, she did start to feel better. She liked the room so much she almost forgot how scared she was. But when the council members filed in to take their seats, her stomach started jumping again.

God, she prayed, *help me not be so scared.*

Megan's mom explained everything that was happening. When it was Megan's turn to talk she squeezed her hand and said, "Go on, Megan. Speak up nice and loud."

There was a podium at the front of the center aisle. Megan took the petition to it and Brooke stood next to her while she spoke into the microphone. "My name is Megan Hicks," she told the city council, "and I live in Parkwood sub-division." Megan looked at her dad who gave her a thumbs-up. She took a deep breath and turned back to the microphone. "We have a tree on Grace Street," she said. "It's an oak tree, and it's over two hundred years old. It has owls in it," she added. Megan tried to swallow but her mouth was too dry.

The chairman of the city council leaned forward and raised his bushy eyebrows. "Yes?"

"Well, it's about the sidewalks," said Megan. "We're glad we're getting sidewalks, but we need to keep the trees."

"I see." The chairman nodded and sat back against the brown leather cushion of his chair. "But I don't know how we can manage that if the trees are in the way of the sidewalks."

"That's what I thought," said Megan. "Then I thought, Why can't the sidewalks go *around* the trees? And then we said, 'Let's make a petition.'" Megan grabbed Brooke's arm and pulled her closer to the front of the microphone. "Tell about the petition."

"We made a petition," said Brooke. She gathered up the stack of yellow paper from the podium and held it high. "We have over a thousand names."

"Would you read your petition for the record, please," said the chairman. "Then hand it over to the clerk."

Brooke did.

The clerk smiled at them as he took the petition. He carried it to the chairman who smiled at them as he passed it down the table. Each of the members smiled at them as the petition went by. But that was all. The chairman thanked them for all their hard work and said the council would think about it.

"They're not going to do it, are they?" said Megan when they were on their way home.

"They said they'd think about it," said her dad.

"But they won't, will they?" said Brooke.

Mr. Allen sighed. He reached across the back of the seat and took his daughter's hand. "No, Megs," he said, "I'm afraid they won't."

Chapter Six

On Wednesday, Megan expected a bad day and she got one. All the kids at school wanted to know about the city council meeting, but Megan nearly cried when she even thought about it. "They said they'd think it over," she told them, and then rushed away before they could ask any more questions.

Even Mr. Vanatta, when he was handing out permission slips for a field trip on Monday, said,

"Well, Megan, how is that petition coming along?" Megan didn't know he'd even heard about the petition.

At dinner Megan announced, "I don't want to go to Junior Fellowship tonight."

Her mom and dad looked at one another. "I like Fellowship," said Amy. "We get to make things."

Megan's mom smiled at Amy, but her dad looked straight at Megan. "We don't always succeed at everything we try to do, Megan. That's just the way things are, and we can't stop living our lives because we've failed at something."

Megan could tell her dad was disappointed in her because he didn't call her Megs. "I didn't say I wanted to stop going," she told him. "I just don't want to go tonight."

"Well, I think it would be a good idea."

"Maybe it would make you feel better," said her mom.

At church that night, Megan and Brooke sat in a corner and tried to be invisible, but Mrs. Farmer started the meeting by saying, "First, let's find out how the petition is going. Megan? Brooke? Who wants to tell us about it?"

Brooke looked at Megan. Megan looked at her shoes. Brooke said, "We got lots of names, and we took the petition to the city council meeting last night. The members said they'd think about it."

Mrs. Farmer was smiling broadly. "That's wonderful," she said.

"No it isn't," said Megan suddenly. "They just said that. They won't really think about it."

"You don't know that, Megan," Mrs. Farmer said gently.

"Yes I do. They all smiled when they looked at our petition. They just thought it was cute because we're kids."

"Like Goliath when David met him in battle with only a sling and a stone."

Megan looked up at Mrs. Farmer. "Goliath?"

"Don't you remember? He laughed. Goliath was over nine feet tall. Not a soldier in Saul's army was brave enough to face him. And there was David, who was just a boy, standing there ready to fight him. Goliath must have thought it was some kind of joke."

"But it wasn't," said Megan firmly.

"It certainly wasn't, Megan," agreed Mrs. Farmer. "David wasn't laughing, and he wasn't afraid. Why? What did he know that Goliath didn't?"

"He was really good with that sling," suggested Michael.

"That's true," said Mrs. Farmer. "To protect his sheep, he had killed lions and bears with it. What else?"

"He knew God was helping him," said Brooke.

Mrs. Farmer smiled. "Actually, to David, it was more like he was helping God. But you're right, Brooke. He knew God was with him."

It was Mr. Allen's turn to pick them up from church. On the way home Amy showed everyone what she had made in class, and Michael told his dad that their group had spent a lot of time talking about the petition.

Mr. Allen asked, "Have you decided what you are going to do next?"

"About what?" asked Brooke.

"About saving the trees, of course. You're not going to stop now, are you?"

"But what else can we do?" asked Megan. "They won't listen to us. We're just kids."

"David was just a kid," Michael reminded her.

"That's right," said Mr. Allen, "and so was

Joan of Arc when she led the armies of France against Britain."

"But they were fighting for God," said Megan.

They had just turned into Megan's driveway, and Mr. Allen stopped the car and looked at her. "Aren't you?" he asked. "Aren't you fighting for God's trees because God's creatures need them?"

"I guess so," said Megan, "but I don't know what else to do."

"You just keep praying," he told her, "and do what you feel God is asking you to do."

Megan thanked him and helped Amy get out of the car. She watched the Allens back out and pull into their own driveway down the street. She looked at the Owl Tree.

"Come on," said Amy, pulling at her sleeve.

"You go ahead," she told Amy. Megan was thinking about David and how Mrs. Farmer had said he was helping God. Megan realized that she hadn't prayed about the trees since Brooke came up with the idea of a petition. *I haven't even been asking God to help me,* she thought. *I've been trying to do it all by myself.*

"Megan?" Her dad came down the walk and stood beside her.

"God wants the trees to be saved, Dad."

"You think so?"

"Yes."

Megan's dad put his arm around her shoulders and they stood there looking at the Owl Tree together. After a moment Megan continued, "God made the trees for us, but He expects us to take care of them."

"I think you're right, Megs." Megan smiled just a little when he called her Megs. "You remember that puppy your Uncle Harry gave you?"

"Ben?" asked Megan. She had almost forgotten about Ben.

"Your mom and I didn't think you were old enough, but you promised that you would take care of him."

"But I didn't, did I," Megan remembered, "and we had to give him back."

"That was the deal."

Megan thought about puppies and trees. "Well, I'm older now," she said, "and I'm going to help God take care of the trees."

Megan's dad didn't say anything, but he squeezed her shoulders in a little sideways hug.

"Dad?"

"Hmm?"

"I'm glad I went to Junior Fellowship tonight."

"That's my girl," he said, and he ruffled Megan's hair.

On Friday, Megan went to Brooke's house after school. They found cookies and lemonade in the kitchen, and took the snack to the big swing on the front porch. Megan nibbled around a chocolate chip and watched the Owl Tree. "The eggs haven't hatched," she said.

"The owls' eggs?" asked Brooke.

Megan nodded. "They've usually hatched by now. I hope nothing's wrong with them."

"Maybe it would be better if they didn't have babies this year," said Brooke.

Megan looked at Brooke with wide eyes. "Why?"

"Well, you know, if they cut the tree down . . ."

"They are not going to cut down the Owl Tree," Megan said firmly.

"But the petition didn't work."

"Then we'll just have to think of something else."

"What?"

"I don't know yet." Megan's forehead wrinkled as she thought, and she silently asked God to give them an idea.

Brooke said, "Maybe we could write a letter."

"Who to?"

"I don't know. I was just thinking about that girl in California who wrote to the president of Russia. Maybe we could write to our president."

"I don't think so," said Megan. "They'd probably have the trees cut down before he even had time to read the letter."

"Yeah."

Josh and his skateboard came roaring up the driveway and down the walk. "Cookies?" he asked, looking hungrily at the plate that sat between Megan and Brooke.

Brooke offered him the plate and said, "But if you take our cookies, you have to help us think."

Josh pick up three cookies at once. "About what?" he asked.

"About saving the trees," said Megan.

"Oh," said Josh, and he munched quietly for a moment.

"We thought about writing a letter," Brooke told him, "but we don't know where to send it."

"Hey, yeah," said Josh. "You know that billboard out on Memorial Drive? The one about kids wanting grown-ups to be nicer to the environment?"

"It's great, Josh," said Megan, "but billboards cost a lot of money."

"Not that one. A girl in Tennessee wrote a letter to an advertising agency and asked them to put one up, so they did. Then they talked about it on television and other agencies all across the country started putting up the same billboard. There are hundreds of them now."

"Wow," said Brooke.

"That's it!" Megan said. "That's who we'll send our letter to."

"Who?" said Brooke. "An advertising agency?"

"No, a television station. All the television stations. And all the radio stations, and the newspapers, too. Josh, you're a genius."

Josh shrugged. "Of course," he said, and grabbed another cookie.

Chapter Seven

Dear News Person,
We are the kids from
Grace Street in Parkwood
subdevision. The City is
going to cut down our trees
so we can have sidewalks.
We want them to put the
sidewalks around the trees
so we can have birds and
skwirls too.

"Is that how you spell squirrels?" asked Brooke. She was leaning against Megan's left shoulder, and Josh was hanging over the back of the swing.

Megan looked at them, then back at the letter in her lap. "Squirrels," she said slowly, listening to the sounds. "I don't know. Do you think there's an *e* in it?"

"I think there's a *q* in it," said Josh. "You got a dictionary, Brooksie?"

While Brooke went inside for the dictionary, Megan tried to think of something else to write. "Should we tell them about the owls?" she asked Josh.

"You already said birds," he pointed out. "Maybe you should tell them about the petition."

We made a pitition and over a 1000 people signed it. But the City counsel didn't care because we are just kids.

Megan nodded and bent over her paper again. "What else?" asked Megan, taking the dictionary from Brooke and handing her the letter to read.

"We'd better say why we're writing them," suggested Josh.

"Why are we writing them?" asked Brooke.

Josh poked Brooke's shoulder with his fist. "Because we want them to help, dummy."

"I'm not a dummy," said Brooke, rubbing her shoulder. "I know we want their help, but what are we asking them to do?"

They looked at each other for a moment. No one knew the answer to Brooke's question. Finally Megan said, "How 'bout if we just ask them to help and let them figure out what to do?"

Brooke and Josh nodded agreement. Megan reached for the letter and wrote:

Please can you help us stop the City from cutting down our trees?

"We can get the addresses from the phone book," said Megan, "and we'll have to make copies for every station and every newspaper."

"We'll help," said Brooke.

"And we can all sign them," said Josh.

"Let's get Michael and Georgie and Marty to sign, too," suggested Megan.

"Then they can help copy," said Brooke.

Brooke went to find her brother and sister while Josh helped Megan check her spelling in the dictionary. By dinnertime, all the letters were copied, signed, folded, and stuffed into envelopes, ready to mail. It had taken the last of Megan's allowance to buy stamps. Marty was at her grandmother's for the weekend, Josh didn't get an allowance, and the Allens wouldn't get their allowances until Sunday night.

"I'll give you some money for stamps on Monday," said Brooke, as they walked to the mailbox after dinner. "All I have left is my tithe."

"That's OK," said Megan. Megan got her allowance on Saturdays so she could give her tithe to the church right away. She was glad she didn't have to wait a whole week and be tempted to spend it.

"Hey," said Brooke suddenly, "we have a field trip Monday."

"Hey, yeah." Megan had forgotten, too. "Are you going?"

"You kidding? My dad loves it when we go to museums and stuff. Is this the one with the pictures and statues, or is it the good one?"

Megan said, "It's the Museum of Natural History."

"Does it have animals in it?"

"Of course it does. It's about nature."

"That's the good one," said Brooke.

Megan laughed, but secretly she agreed. The Museum of Natural History was her favorite "serious" place to go. They had dinosaur bones and lots of animals that were stuffed and set up in little scenes so you could see how the real ones lived. You weren't allowed to touch those, but they had some in the Children's Room that you could pet. Megan always liked to go there first.

On Monday, they didn't get to the Children's Room until after lunch. The museum guide, wearing a badge that said his name was Mark, held the door open while Mr. Vanatta herded the class into the room.

"We have something new in the Children's Room today," said Mark, as he squeezed past them to a shelf on the far wall. Megan moved around until she could see. Her mouth flew open, and she grabbed Brooke's arm.

"Ow!" said Brooke, and Mr. Vanatta gave them a stern look.

"It's one of the owls," whispered Megan. Then Brooke saw it, too, perched on an oak limb, its eyes as wide and unblinking as Megan's were at that moment.

"This fine fellow is a great horned owl," said Mark. "We have only had the pleasure of his company since last week."

Megan tried to remember when she last heard the owls on Grace Street.

"We don't see very many owls of this type around here any more," Mark continued. "That's why we feel very fortunate to have gotten this one."

Megan swallowed hard, and asked, "How did he die?"

Mark smiled at her. "Someone shot him, I'm afraid, but now he will be here for all of you to look at and to pet."

"Where?" asked Megan. "Where did they shoot him?"

"What do you mean?"

Mark was frowning now, and Mr. Vanatta was giving Megan a curious look, but Megan didn't care. She said, "I mean, where was he living when they shot him?"

Mark walked over to Megan. His voice was very firm but low when he said, "Why do you want to know?"

"We have owls like that on Grace Street," Megan told him.

"You do?" Mark's voice sounded as though he couldn't believe her. "Well, this owl came from another state. Did you think it was one of your owls?"

Megan nodded. "I'm sorry if I frightened you," Mark said. "Will you tell me about your owls?"

Megan nodded again. Mark told the rest of the class they could look around at the exhibits and ask questions if they wanted to. Then he led her over to the great horned owl.

"Are you sure your owls look just like this one?" he asked.

Megan touched the feathery "horns" and ran the back of her hand across the soft, downy chest. "I'm sure," she said.

"And there are two of them?" asked Mark. "They usually live in pairs."

"They sing in perfect harmony," said Megan.

"I know," said Mark. "Have you ever seen any babies?"

Megan frowned. "Not this year," she said, and looked at Mark earnestly. "Do you think there's something wrong with the eggs?"

Mark said, "I don't know. Did they have babies last year?"

"Three," Megan told him, proudly.

"Then they must be pretty good parents," said Mark. "I don't think I'd start worrying just yet."

"But they should be hatched by now."

"I know. Horned owls usually lay their eggs in the winter, but do you remember how cold our winter was this year?"

Megan nodded. "We used up all our snow days at school."

"I think maybe your owls just got started a little late this time," said Mark. "What do you think?"

Megan could only say, "I hope so," before Mr. Vanatta started lining everyone up at the door.

"Let's go, class," he said, motioning to the

group. "There are three more classes that have to get in here before we leave today."

Megan broke into line behind Brooke. As soon as Mr. Vanatta was out of range, Brooke spun around to face her and whispered excitedly, "Well? What did he say?"

"Who?"

"Who? The guide, that's who. What did you talk about?"

"You know what we talked about."

"The owls?"

Megan nodded, and Brooke looked disappointed.

"What did you think we talked about?" Megan asked her.

"I don't know, but all the girls think he's so cute, and they were all so jealous they couldn't stand it."

"They were?" said Megan. The line was moving out, but she turned and walked backward, trying to get another look at Mark.

After school, they went to Megan's house. "I can't believe you didn't think he was cute," said Brooke, when they were in the privacy of Megan's room.

"I didn't say that," Megan told her. "I said I didn't notice."

"That's even worse," exclaimed Brooke.

"No it isn't," said Megan. "Anyway, he's a grown-up."

"Grown-ups can be cute."

Megan grabbed a stuffed bear and was about to sail it across the room at Brooke when there was a knock on the door. Megan put the bear behind her and called, "Come in."

Megan's mom opened the door and stuck her head in. "Megan, come quick," she said, and her voice sounded hushed and excited. "It's the telephone. Somebody from a television station. She wants to talk to you."

Chapter Eight

"We're going to be on TV-e-e-e!"

The end of Megan's sentence rose upward into a high-pitched squeal as she hung up the phone. Brooke grabbed her, and the two jumped up and down in a little circular dance. Megan gave her mom a bear hug.

"When?" asked Brooke. "When are they coming?"

"Tomorrow. After school. It's OK, isn't it, Mom?"

"I gave them my permission before they talked to you."

Megan hugged her again, and looked at Brooke. The girls grinned at each other for a moment, before squealing and dancing around some more.

The next day Megan's mom picked them up at school. Megan was so excited she bounced on the seat until her mom quieted her with a hand on her knee. Michael teased Brooke about being a television star, but Georgie and Marty seemed happier about not having to ride the bus than about anything else.

When the Eyewitness News van pulled into Megan's driveway, all the Grace Street Kids were there except Josh O'Grady.

"Where's Josh?" asked Michael, but no one answered because just then a man and woman were climbing out of the van.

The man wore a blue suit with a red, white, and blue tie, and he carried a small notebook. The woman wore jeans and a blue jacket that said Eyewitness News across the back. From the side of the van she pulled a large camera, swung it to her shoulder, and followed the man up the walk. Megan's mom stepped out to meet them.

"I'm Mrs. Hicks," she said. "This is Megan." She put her hand on Megan's back and gently pulled Megan over in front of her.

"Russ Pelham," said the man. He shook hands with Megan's mom and smiled at Megan. "Hello, Megan."

"Hello," said Megan. With her mom's hands resting on her shoulders Megan felt brave. "Thank you for coming," she added.

"You're welcome," said Russ Pelham. "We liked your letter very much."

Megan smiled shyly, and her mom introduced the other kids to the reporter. He had them all stand in Megan's yard with Megan in front and the Owl Tree behind them. The woman with the camera handed him a microphone, which he pointed at Megan.

"Don't worry about this," he said. "You just talk to me, OK?"

"OK."

Russ Pelham looked at the woman, who nodded and then squinted into the eyepiece. He turned back to Megan. "Now, I want you to start at the beginning, and tell me just what you told us in your letter. Can you do that?"

"Yes."

"Great. We're all set, so you just go ahead and start whenever you're ready."

Megan told him about the sidewalks, about the bright orange X's on the trees, and about the petition to make the sidewalks curve around. "Mr. Allen says they have curvy sidewalks in Atlanta," she added.

"What did the city council say about your petition?"

"They said they would think about it."

"But they won't," said Brooke.

Russ Pelham pointed the microphone at Brooke. "What makes you think that?" he asked.

"We're just kids," she told him. "Grown-ups don't listen to kids."

"I'm listening," said Russ Pelham. "What are you going to do next, if the city goes ahead with its plans?"

Megan had been thinking about that, ever since she found out she was going to be on TV. She had been praying about it, too, and she knew what she wanted to say.

"We want everyone to call the city council," she began, but Russ Pelham wasn't listening any more. Megan could hear the grinding of skateboard wheels on the pavement behind her. Michael whispered, "Josh," and everyone looked toward the Owl Tree. The woman with the camera moved around them and pointed the lens at the old oak where Josh O'Grady was tying a giant, red STOP sign to the trunk. Megan had seen the sign before, on the door to Josh's room. He also had a giant, yellow YIELD sign above his bed and a traffic light lamp in the corner that flashed red, yellow, and green.

"Who is that?" asked Russ Pelham.

"Josh O'Grady," Megan told him, and he wrote the name in his notebook.

Josh mounted his skateboard and shoved off, making two or three fancy turns before roaring up Megan's driveway and skidding to a stop in front of the camera. Brooke was scowling at him, but Megan had to smile. He had just given her a super-duper whopper of an idea.

Russ Pelham took the microphone over to Josh and asked, "Why did you put up that sign? What does it mean?"

"Well," said Josh, "it means 'stop,' don't cut down this tree."

"It means 'S.T.O.P. — Save the Trees of Parkwood,'" said Megan, "and we're going to cover up every single one of those big, orange X's with more signs just like that."

The kids all cheered.

Russ Pelham asked Megan a few more questions before the Eyewitness News team started packing up their van.

"When will this be on?" asked Megan.

"Tonight at ten," said Russ Pelham.

Megan and Amy were allowed to stay up past their bedtimes to watch. Russ Pelham stood in front of a row of trees on Parkwood Boulevard and explained what all the X's meant. When he talked about S.T.O.P., they saw Josh putting that huge sign on Mrs. Jenson's oak. Then they saw the kids cheering, and it looked like they were cheering for Josh.

"Where's Megan?" asked Amy.

"He didn't even say we live on Grace Street," Megan complained.

"Sometimes," said her mom, "they have to

take parts of the story out because they don't have enough time for all of it."

Megan stammered, "But—but all that stuff I told him, and they only showed Josh."

Megan's dad leaned forward in his chair and looked at her. "It seems to me," he said, "that they got in all the basic facts about what you kids are trying to do. Now, which is more important to you, Megan—that people find out about what's happening to the trees or that you be on television?"

"I know," said Megan. "I just thought . . ." She trailed off because she didn't want to tell him what she had thought, how she had looked forward to being a hero tomorrow at school.

He said, "Come here." Megan went to stand in front of him and his face softened as he looked at her. "We all feel jealous sometimes, Megs, but you can't let it get hold of you. You have to ask God to help you get over it. You understand?"

Megan nodded and her dad smiled and whispered. "That's my girl," then asked for a hug. Megan hugged him, and her mom announced, "Hugs for everyone. It's bedtime, girls."

When Megan said her prayers before climbing

into bed, she thanked God for the super-duper whopper of an idea He had sent her, then added, "Please help me not be jealous of Josh."

At school the next day she had to pray that part again, and again, and again. Megan thought every kid in the sixth grade must have seen Josh on the news.

When lunch came, Josh carried his tray to Megan's table. "Isn't it great, Hiccups?"

"Don't call me Hiccups," said Megan irritably.

Josh looked hurt. "You mad at me, Megan?"

"You know I don't like that silly nickname."

"OK. I'm sorry."

Megan was, too. "Isn't what great?" she asked.

"Everybody wants to help," said Josh. "With S.T.O.P."

"They do?"

"Yeah. That was really good, when you came up with Save the Trees of Parkwood."

"Well, the sign was your idea."

While they finished their lunch, Josh and Megan made plans. They decided to ask all the kids in their class to make S.T.O.P. signs and put them up on their streets. The ones who didn't live in Parkwood could bring their signs to someone who did. By Saturday they would have every X covered up.

Megan forgot all about being jealous. She spent the afternoon spreading the word about the signs. Josh was right. Everyone wanted to help.

"It's going to work, Brooke," said Megan as they stepped off the bus at Grace Street. "I just know it."

"Well it was your idea," said Brooke, "not Josh's."

"I don't even care whose idea it was. I'm just so happy that it's going to work." Megan hugged her books to her chest and spun around.

Brooke laughed. "I hope so. Let's go to my house and make our signs."

"OK." Megan stopped suddenly and looked at Brooke. "You think Mrs. Farmer will let us make signs at Junior Fellowship tonight?"

"I bet she will," said Brooke.

Suddenly, Mrs. Jenson burst out her front door and rushed down the walk shouting, "Megan! Megan, come here!"

Megan ran to meet her. "What is it?" she asked. "What's wrong?"

"Nothing!" Mrs. Jenson leaned on Megan's shoulder and took some deep breaths. "Megan, they've hatched," she said finally.

"The owls?" said Megan, and Mrs. Jenson nodded. "The babies have hatched?"

"This morning."

"How many?" asked Megan.

"Only two this time."

Megan said, "Thanks, Mrs. Jenson," and grabbed Brooke's arm. "Come on."

They ran to Josh's house, almost beating him to the back door. "What's up?" he asked.

"We've got to see the owls," said Megan. "The babies have hatched."

Chapter Nine

Josh's room had the best view on Grace Street of the owls' nest. His room was on the second story at the front of the house, and you could climb out his window onto the porch roof and look right over at the top of the Owl Tree.

"I can't see," said Brooke. "Let me have those."

She reached for Josh's binoculars, but he pulled away. "Wait your turn," he said.

"Well, don't hog them."

103

"I can't see anything, anyway," said Josh, but he turned his back to Brooke and handed the binoculars to Megan. "You try."

Megan put them to her eyes and focused. She saw one owl perched on a limb, its sleepy eyes turned toward the nest. The other owl was standing over the nest poking food down the throats of two fluffy gray babies. With their eyes still closed and their legs covered in fuzzy down, Megan thought the owlets looked more like kittens than birds.

"Can you see anything?" asked Josh.

"They're beautiful."

"It's my turn," said Brooke, taking the binoculars.

Megan looked at Josh. "We *can't* let them cut down the trees now," she said. "There are babies. We've got to stop them."

"We will," said Josh.

By Friday afternoon, almost every tree that was marked for destruction had been adopted by one of their classmates. As the school bus followed its route through Parkwood subdivision, Megan saw bright red S.T.O.P. signs all along the way. "Look at all of them," she told Brooke.

"I know," said Brooke, "and we're just getting started."

"The city council will have to change its mind now," said Megan.

Megan went home long enough to throw her books in her room and grab her dad's binoculars. She tried to sneak past Amy's room, but Amy caught her when she was halfway across the kitchen.

"I want to go, too."

"I took you yesterday," Megan told her.

"I want to go again," Amy said stubbornly.

"I won't be gone that long," Megan began, but stopped when Brooke came crashing in the back door.

"Megan, it's him," she said between breaths. "He's over at Josh's."

"Who?" asked Megan.

"The guide. The cute one. From the museum."

"Mark?"

"The one you talked to in the Children's Room."

"What's he doing at Josh's?"

"Watching the owls," said Brooke.

Megan and Brooke took off, leaving Amy standing in the kitchen, and ran to Josh's house. Mrs. O'Grady let them in. "Josh is already up there," she told them.

"And the man from the museum?" asked Brooke.

"He came by right after lunch," said Mrs. O'Grady. "Why anyone would want to spend the entire weekend watching a bunch of owls, I'll never know, but I told him it would be OK."

Megan and Brooke grinned at one another and went up to Josh's room. When they climbed out on the porch roof, Mark said, "Hello, Megan."

"You remember me?" Megan asked.

"Of course. You're the one who told me about these magnificent owls. How could I forget?"

Megan smiled shyly, and Mark added, "I see the babies finally hatched."

"Two of them," said Megan.

Mark looked through a very large lens that was mounted on a tripod. It looked like a telescope, except it had a camera attached. "The male must be out hunting," he said.

Megan looked through her binoculars at the owls.

Brooke asked Mark, "How did you know to come here?"

"Well, Megan said you lived on Grace Street, and I knew if you had owls they had to be in the top of that old oak over there. This was the best place for watching them."

Josh laughed. "He just came up to the door and asked Mom if he could climb out on our roof. You should have seen her face!"

They all laughed then, until Mark said, "Shh, he's back," and put his eye up to the camera. Josh and Megan looked through their binoculars, and Brooke kept squinting her eyes at the Owl Tree and whispering, "Let me see."

With a field mouse clutched in his talons, one of the owls sailed in to a branch near the nest. He took the mouse in his beak and walked the branch like a tightrope, one foot in front of the other, until he reached the nest. The other owl took the mouse and, holding it with her talons, tore off small pieces for the wide-open mouths of the babies in front of her.

"The male does all the hunting when the owlets are this small," said Mark between the clicks of his camera's shutter. "The female stays to guard the nest."

Having delivered the mouse, the male backed off down the limb, puffed out his chest, and watched the babies eat. "I think he's proud of himself," said Megan.

Mark laughed, and Brooke said, "Will someone *please* let me see?"

Megan handed Brooke her binoculars. Even without them, she could see the male take off again and fly toward the farmland on the other side of the creek that bordered Parkwood subdivision.

"There he goes," said Josh. "I guess the babies are still hungry."

"The babies stay hungry," said Mark, "all the time. They've got a lot of growing to do."

"Me, too," declared Josh. "You guys want some chips or something?"

"Sure," agreed Brooke, and Josh headed for the kitchen.

Mark sat back against the side of the house and looked at Megan. "I never did thank you," he said, "for telling me about the owls."

"I can't believe you came all the way out here to look at them," said Megan.

"I wanted to study them," explained Mark. He showed the girls his notebook. He had written down everything the owls had done since he started watching them. "I may even write a paper about their habits if I can get enough information."

"If the city doesn't kill them first," said Brooke.

"What do you mean?"

"The city is going to build sidewalks," said Brooke.

"And they want to cut down the Owl Tree," said Megan, "but we're going to stop them."

Brooke said, "S.T.O.P., as in Save the Trees of Parkwood. That was Megan's idea."

"That explains all those S.T.O.P. signs I saw on my way over here," said Mark.

"We're going to make the city council put the sidewalks around the trees," Megan told him.

"Good for you," Mark said. "There just may be something I can do . . ."

Mark was interrupted when Josh stuck the top half of his body through the window and handed Megan a bag of apples. "This is all I could get," he told them. "Mom said it's too close to dinnertime." Then he ducked back inside and came out onto the roof feet first.

"Apples are great," said Mark.

They munched apples and watched the owls until Megan and Brooke went home for dinner.

On Saturday Megan was up early, but she didn't go to Josh's until she saw Mr. O'Grady retrieving his newspaper from behind the nandina bushes. "Good thing he didn't put it on the roof," he said with a wink. "Might've hit that young fellow right in the head."

"Is Mark already up there?" asked Megan.

"He's been up there all night," said Mr. O'Grady.

Mrs. O'Grady made Megan sit down and eat some toast with them while Josh finished his breakfast. When they got upstairs, they found Mark sitting on a sleeping bag, eating a granola bar, and writing in his notebook.

"What are they doing?" Megan asked.

"Good morning," said Mark. "They're asleep right now."

Josh said, "That's good, because Mom said to tell you to come down for breakfast."

"That's nice of her," Mark protested, "but I don't expect you to feed me while I'm here. It's enough that you're letting me be here."

"You don't know Mrs. O'Grady," said Megan. "She'll get her feelings hurt if you don't go down."

Josh nodded. "Mom loves to have company."

"Well maybe I am a little hungry," said Mark, and he went downstairs for breakfast.

Megan and Josh watched the owls sleep. After a while, Megan turned her binoculars toward the creek to look for songbirds. Black and white cattle were grazing in the field beyond.

"Did our neighborhood used to have cows in it?" she wondered.

Josh said, "No, Dad told me it used to be Parker's Woods. That's where they got the name Parkwood."

"Oh. I bet the owls liked it better when it was all trees."

"Look at that," Josh said suddenly. He had turned his binoculars in the other direction, toward Parkwood Boulevard. "They're putting up S.T.O.P. signs down by the fire hall."

When Megan scooted around to look, she saw

something else that made her suck in a quick breath. "No, they can't," she cried, and scrambled in through Josh's window.

"Megan?" Josh saw her run through his room and start down the steps, and then he leaned out over the roof's railing to get a better view of Grace Street. A city road crew was pulling up beside the Owl Tree, and they had chain saws in the back of the truck.

Chapter Ten

Megan put herself between the Owl Tree and the city road worker. He was a tall man with big muscles, but Megan stood still and looked him in the eye. He let the chain saw swing down by his side and shook his head. "We haven't got time for games, kid."

"This isn't a game," said Megan, in a voice that was loud and strong.

"You've got that right," said the worker, and took a step toward her.

"Don't you lay a hand on that child!" Mrs. Jenson came hurrying down her walk, right arm outstretched and index finger pointing fiercely.

The road worker's partner climbed from the cab of the truck and rushed over. "She's right, Joe. I've radioed the base to call the police. Let them handle it."

The man called Joe glared at Megan for a moment. He turned back to the truck and angrily shoved the chain saw into the bed.

"Megan Dolores Hicks!" Megan heard the voice before she saw her mom come charging across the street, Amy at her heels. "What in the world do you think you're doing?"

"They can't cut it down, Mom. We can't let them."

Josh grabbed Megan's right hand. "She's right, Mrs. Hicks."

Amy tried to hold Megan's left hand, but her mom pulled her back. "Megan, are you sure you know what you're getting yourself into?"

Megan nodded.

"We all do," said Brooke.

Megan looked around. Grace Street Kids were coming from all directions. Brooke took Megan's left hand. Michael held Brooke's left hand, and Georgie held Michael's. Marty slipped in between Georgie and Josh, and they formed a ring around the trunk of the oak.

All along Grace Street, people were coming out to their front yards to see what all the fuss was about. By the time the police arrived, the neighbors had crowded in until there was a second, larger ring enclosing the tree and the city truck. The officer had to sound a blast on her siren in order to get the patrol car through. An Eyewitness News van followed her in.

"Look!" said Megan. "It's Russ Pelham."

"They listen to police calls on the radio," explained Josh. "I'm sure glad they heard this one."

The police officer got out of the car. She slid her nightstick into its place on her belt as she walked over to the city truck. Her partner got out, too, but stayed by the car.

"What have we got here?" she asked Joe.

His partner answered. "They don't want the tree cut down," he said mildly.

"And we got orders to cut it down," added Joe.

The officer turned and looked at the kids

ringing the big oak like a string of paper dolls. Russ Pelham stuck a microphone in her face and asked, "Are you going to forcibly remove the children?"

She glared at him, said, "Get that thing out of my face," and went over to the kids. She set her cap back a little on her head and smiled at Megan. "Hi. I hear you don't want these men to cut down this tree. Is that right?"

Megan nodded.

The officer took a step back and looked up at the old oak. "It is a beautiful tree. I can understand why you don't want it cut down. What's your name?"

"Megan Hicks."

"Well, Megan, can you understand that these men are just trying to do their jobs?"

"Yes."

"But you're not going to move."

"No."

The officer nodded thoughtfully and walked back to the city truck. Megan looked around. Mrs. Jenson was standing nearby smiling encouragement at them. Her mom and Amy were next to Mrs. Jenson. Her mom looked worried.

Mr. and Mrs. O'Grady were just across the street. Mr. O'Grady winked when he saw Megan looking.

Among the other familiar faces of the Grace Street neighbors were faces she had never seen before.

"Who are all these people?"

Josh said, "Maybe they listen to police calls, too."

"That lady over there by your mom lives on Belle Road," said Brooke. "She signed the petition."

The police officer had been talking with the road crew. Megan saw her smile and pat Joe on the back. The officer started toward the Owl Tree, and Russ Pelham fell into step beside her.

"What are you going to do?"

The officer stopped and looked at him "The road crew has received instructions to move to another location. They'll come back here when it isn't quite so crowded," she added with a little smile.

Russ Pelham smiled back. "Which location? Our dispatcher tells us that there are children protecting trees all over Parkwood subdivision."

Josh let out a whoop and the other kids cheered. Megan asked, "How did they know?"

Marty leaned around the tree. "I called Jeffrey Tucker before I came over and told him to call some of the others."

The two men in the road crew huddled beside the city truck. The two police officers huddled beside the patrol car. Russ Pelham and his camera crew huddled beside the Eyewitness News van. Megan watched carefully to see what would happen next.

"Uh-oh," said Josh.

"What?" But when Megan turned to look at him she knew. Her dad's car was pulling over in front of Josh's house. Her dad walked straight to Megan.

"What's going on here, Megs?"

"We're protecting the Owl Tree," she told him.

"I see."

"Mr. Hicks?" The police officer walked up beside Megan's dad.

"Yes."

"Megan and her friends are upset over losing their favorite climbing tree," she began.

"There's a little more to it than that," said

Megan's dad. "My daughter believes very strongly that it would be wrong to cut down this tree."

"It wouldn't just be wrong," said Mark, pushing between Mr. O'Grady and another man. "It would be tragic. There are two owlets up there that will die if this tree is cut down now."

The officer turned to Mark. "Who are you?"

"Mark Collins. I'm with the Museum of Natural History."

Russ Pelham crowded in and pushed his microphone toward Mark. "Isn't your father Geoffrey Collins, president of the city council?"

"Yes, and I've just spoken with my father," said Mark. "He has agreed to call an emergency meeting of the city council on Monday night to take another look at Megan's petition."

A cheer went up around the tree. Parents and neighbors rushed in to congratulate the kids. The road crew left. The police officer went to her patrol car and called someone on the radio. Russ Pelham talked to Mark about the owls.

Megan found her mom and dad standing with the Allens in Mrs. Jenson's front yard. She gave them each a hug and said, "Thank you."

Her dad asked, "What for?"

"For not getting mad."

He looked at her. "Why did you do it, Megs?"

"To save the Owl Tree."

"I know, but why?"

Megan thought about it. *The earth is the Lord's*, she remembered. Aloud, she said, "Because God wants us to take care of the things He gave us."

Her dad smiled and ruffled her hair. "How could we be mad about that?"

Megan smiled back, and decided her dad was the most wonderful person in the world. Then she thought of something. "Do I have to talk to the city council again?"

"I think you should be the one to tell them about the baby owls." he said.

"And I think," said Mr. Allen, "that it's time the grown-ups did some talking, too."

He and Megan's dad walked off toward the Allens' house, talking quietly together. Amy hugged Megan's waist.

"Weren't you scared, Megan?"

"I didn't think about it," said Megan.

"I certainly was," said her mom. She smoothed Megan's hair and added, "But I was very proud of you."

"Megan's a hero." said Amy.

As if on cue, Mrs. Jenson hurried over. "Megan, there you are. Those television people are looking for you."

That night when the story aired on the news, there was no question about who had saved the Owl Tree from the chain saw. Megan was right out front, and at church on Sunday, and at school on Monday, Megan was a hero.

"It was Mark who got the city council to meet again," she reminded them.

"But you stopped those men while he was doing that," said Brooke.

"Not just me. We all did."

Josh said, "Yeah, but you went out there first, all by yourself."

Everyone agreed with Josh and patted her on the back. Megan felt proud, but she knew she had only been able to do it because she was helping God. She also knew there was another battle to be won.

"We haven't really saved the trees," she said, "until the city council changes its mind about the sidewalks."

When members of the city council filed in to take their seats for the called meeting on Monday night, the room was packed. Almost every family on Grace Street was there, as well as a lot of the people Megan had seen standing around the Owl Tree on Saturday morning. And there were a lot more that Megan had never seen. Some of the kids carried large, red S.T.O.P. signs.

Megan's family, the Allens, and the O'Gradys had come early and gotten seats at the front of the room near the podium. Megan's dad wouldn't tell her what he and Mr. Allen had talked about all weekend. He just smiled and said, "You'll see."

Geoffrey Collins banged his gavel and everyone got quiet. He called the meeting to order and explained why they were there. When he said they would hear comments from the floor, Megan went to the podium.

"The oak tree on Grace Street has owls in it," she reminded them. "Now the owls have two babies. If you cut down the tree, the babies will die."

The chairman said, "So I understand, and the

council sees no reason why the tree shouldn't be preserved until the owlets have left the nest."

Mr. Allen stood up. "It should be preserved longer than that," he said. "That oak is over two hundred years old. It is older than our nation. How can we think of cutting it down?"

"And it's not just the Owl Tree," said Megan. "The birds and animals in Parkwood need *all* the trees."

Geoffrey Collins said, "What would you suggest, young lady?" He held up the petition. "This idea of curving the sidewalks is hardly reasonable. It would cost the taxpayers too much money."

Mr. Allen smiled at Megan's dad. Mr. Hicks went to the podium and whispered in Megan's ear, "Here we go," then leaned over the microphone. "If the council will agree to curve the sidewalks around the trees," he told them, "the residents of Parkwood subdivision will pay the difference in the cost."

"Do you speak for the residents of Parkwood?" asked Geoffrey Collins.

Mr. Hicks looked around the room. "Most of them are here tonight. Why don't you ask them?"

A huge cheer went up from the people crowded into the council room. It rattled the windows and lasted until Geoffrey Collins banged his gavel again. He leaned over to talk with the council members on his right, and then he talked with those on his left. They covered their microphones with their hands so no one could hear what they were saying.

Megan tugged at her dad's sleeve and whispered, "What are they doing?"

"They're deciding."

Megan looked at Brooke, who crossed all her fingers, wrapped her arms around one another, and crossed her legs. When she crossed her eyes, Megan giggled.

"Very well," said Geoffrey Collins. "The council is agreed. If the residents of Parkwood will bear the additional expense, we will grant the petition."

The crowd cheered again, and Megan shouted, "What happened?"

"We won!" said her dad, and wrapped Megan in a big hug.

It was like a party. Everyone laughed and hugged each other. Russ Pelham was there. So were reporters from two other television stations, one radio station, and two newspapers. When they got home, Megan and Amy were allowed to stay up for the news, so it was late when Megan finally went to bed.

She waited until her mom had turned off the light and closed the door before getting up and going to the window. She pushed it open and knelt down, resting her arms on the sill. With her eyes on the huge oak, she prayed, "Thank You, God, for saving the Owl Tree. And thank You for letting me help."

Megan thought about the owls. She had wanted to save the tree for them. As it turned out, it was the owls that had saved all the trees of Parkwood. Without them, Mark wouldn't have come to Grace Street, and Megan thought Mark was the real hero.

Megan smiled, said amen, and climbed back into bed. She left the window open so she could go to sleep to the sound of the owls, singing in perfect harmony.